Originally published in Spanish in 2008 as *Mi papá estuvo en la selva*
Text and illustrations © 2008 by Pequeño Editor
Translation © 2020 by Elisa Amado
First published in Canada, the U.S., and the U.K. by Greystone Books in 2020

20 21 22 23 24 5 4 3 2 1

Greystone Kids / Greystone Books Ltd.
greystonebooks.com

An Aldana Libros Book

Cataloguing data available from Library and Archives Canada
ISBN 978-1-77164-670-3 (cloth)
ISBN 978-1-77164-671-0 (epub)

Edited by Patsy Aldana
Copy edited by Antonia Banyard
Proofread by DoEun Kwon
Jacket illustration by Anne Decis
Photographs by Gusti

Printed and bound in Malaysia on ancient-forest-friendly paper by Tien Wah Press

Greystone Books gratefully acknowledges the Musqueam, Squamish, and Tsleil-Waututh peoples on whose land our office is located.

Greystone Books thanks the Canada Council for the Arts, the British Columbia Arts Council, the Province of British Columbia through the Book Publishing Tax Credit, and the Government of Canada for supporting our publishing activities.

by GUSTI   Illustrations by ANNE DECIS
Translated by ELISA AMADO

WHEN MY DAD
WENT TO
THE JUNGLE

AN ALDANA LIBROS BOOK

GREYSTONE KIDS

GREYSTONE BOOKS • VANCOUVER/BERKELEY

One day my dad told me that he had been to the jungle that is the mother of all jungles, with trees so fat and so tall that even if all the kids in my class tried to circle one, we still wouldn't be able to reach all the way around.

But my dad is always exaggerating.

a tarantula can be as big as a plate

The other day when I was going to school, a car drove by and splashed me. Because I was paying attention, I understood that it was a message and I went home.

But my mother didn't agree and sent me back to school.

1, 2, 1, 2…

The thing about eating is incredible … My father is such a picky eater, but he told me that when he was in the jungle, he ate everything they put on his plate, even fish!

He explained to me that because people in the jungle don't have a refrigerator, they smoke the fish to preserve it.

this is how you smoke fish

You can only get there in a small plane. I've never been on any kind of plane, big or small. One time we took a train to my uncle Ignacio's.

in the jungle they also have pets

Dad says that when you travel to a place that's different,
you should always ask for permission before you go and say that
you'll be respectful and that you'll behave. Just like when you
go to a neighbor's house.

And then that place will also respect you.

He told me that gigantic animals live in that jungle.

He didn't see them but he sure heard them.

not all snakes are poisonous

One morning when he was getting dressed, a spider that was as
big as an octopus and very hairy (although octopi don't have hair)
jumped out of his pants.

tarantulas can stick their nails
in and out–like a cat!

My father thanked the jungle because the spider didn't bite him.

He says we have to be very attentive, that there are invisible
messages, and that if you pay attention, you can understand them.

The spider that jumped out of his pants was a message.

I tried it with my friends. We left a kingfish in the window so it would get smoked by the smoke from the cars and buses. After a few days, it smelled so horrible that even the cat wouldn't eat it.

glug, glug, glug

In the jungle, if you're thirsty, you can cut a branch
and delicious water that tastes of herbs comes out of it.

Dad told me that the men hunt to get stuff to eat.

They use a blowgun made from a very, very long hollow reed.
They stick some little arrows into the reed, blow really hard and

ZZUUUUUPP! they shoot.

They almost always hit their target. My dad was so skinny when
he got back that he must have always missed.

yummy
yummy
yummy worms

One of their favorite dishes is big worms called tucus. To eat them, first you have to cut down a palm tree. Then you have to wait a few months for its trunk to fill up with larvae, and then wait a few more weeks for the larvae to turn into big worms. Then you eat them and even make oil out of them.

they also eat hearts of palm from the tucus' tree

My friends and I went into the garden and dug up some earthworms so we could make oil and fry some potatoes. But my mother caught us in the middle of our experiment and almost fainted.

in the jungle four-year-old kids already know how to fish

My dad told me that there are no barbers in the jungle. So the people cut their hair with a piranha fish jaw. Its teeth are as sharp as a saw. They also use them to scratch themselves if they are itchy, or have a bug bite.

I saw photos of my dad with his piranha haircut. Luckily his hair is growing back.

a hand or a foot that stirs up the water can attract a piranha, then ZAP!

My father played lots of volleyball with the people in the jungle.
They bet with chickens on their games.

I bet my dog that I could beat Henry, my fifth-floor neighbor,
in a video game. Because I lost I had to give him Poly,
but his parents got very annoyed and he had to give Poly back.

my Poly

with his dad's machete

Once a week, the people in the jungle get together to make a minga.

That means an activity that all the villagers, small and big, do together.
When my dad was there, they cut down a gigantic tree and then made
a canoe big enough for ten people. (Even my dad worked on it!)

He says that when the families get together, they laugh and sing a lot.
In my house, my parents argue every day, and my mother sings
but only in the shower.

When the rainy season comes, instead of using an umbrella, they cover themselves with big, huge leaves. A whole family can get under one and they won't get wet.

One day when I was going to school, it rained a lot so I covered myself with the leaves from a rubber tree.

I got soaked and, on top of that, my notebook got wet all the way through.

straw roof

laundry line

hen

wood for the fire

Dad told me there is no winter there, that every night
he listened to a frog concert, and that the fireflies were
as bright as fireworks.

Because the houses don't have walls or doors, you can hear the song of the river when you're inside.

One night I left my window open, but all I heard was the sound of cars, and because it was winter, I woke up with a dreadful cold.

Giant eagles live in the jungle. According to the people there, the eagles can imitate the songs of the monkeys. That's how they convince the monkeys to come close to them, then

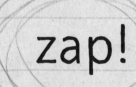 **zap!** they catch them.

"An eagle that eats monkeys?" I thought. So I went to Eduardo's house with a piece of steak. I tried to feed it to his parrot. But the parrot just kept chewing on his sunflower seeds.

hairy blond caterpillar

The eagle that eats monkeys is called a harpy eagle and is the biggest bird in the jungle. The people there respect it very much and consider it a very brave spirit. But people from other places don't care about it and cut down the trees where the eagles have their nests, and also kill the monkeys and other animals that the eagles eat.

My dad told me that harpy eagles are in danger of disappearing.

And he also told me that cows are dangerous for the jungle.

"Cows?" I thought. "With those nice faces?" My dad explained that for each cow they bring to the jungle, they have to cut down lots of trees to grow grass for the cows to eat. That's how the jungle is disappearing little by little.

My dad says that the jungle is a living being that dies and is reborn, and that it is the home for thousands of plants and animals, and that even many spirits live in it.

If I go to the jungle one day, I'll tell the spirits that I love them and ask them to come over one day and eat churros and hot chocolate.

Theo

I went to the jungle in Ecuador in January 2001. I offered to volunteer for a project studying one of the world's most impressive birds—the harpy eagle.

We went to the province of Pastaza, near the border with Peru, to an area called Conambo. That's where the people called the Sápara live. They helped us to find the harpy eagles, which they call *chullwualy* in their language. Ruth Muñiz, an incredible person, is the biologist in charge of the project. This is a very hard job, but she always keeps going. She knows that if there are harpy eagles in one part of the jungle, it will be declared a nature reserve. That would protect it against the indiscriminate cutting of trees, oil drilling, and the loss of the Sápara culture. In fact, the Sápara language is one of the five most endangered languages in the world.

Ruth knows that the presence of the harpy eagle indicates how healthy the forest is. And the more we know about the eagles, the better we can help them to survive.

In my short time in Conambo I was lucky to live with the Sápara and share their way of life a little. I learned so much from them.

PUBLISHER'S NOTE

Amazonia is the vast region of South America that contains the Amazon River and all the smaller waterways that feed into it. Colombia, Peru, Bolivia, Brazil, and Ecuador—where this story takes place—all contain parts of this extraordinary ecosystem. Approximately five thousand Indigenous people live in Amazonia, among them the Sápara. But they and their traditional way of life are endangered. In the early 1900s there were about 200,000 Sápara. Tragically, when Gusti went to stay with them in 2001, only three hundred remained. And Amazonia itself is endangered. Mining, logging, the clearing of land for farms, and the wildfires that result threaten the region's entire ecosystem.

But our planet depends on Amazonia for survival. The billions of trees in the region are essential to absorbing the gases that create global warming. Our oceans and atmosphere also depend on Amazonia. Almost a quarter of our fresh water flows through the Amazon River. And Amazonia is home to the world's largest collection of plant and animal species.

Young people everywhere are protesting global warming, the destruction of our ecosystems, and the impact of both on human life. The more we know about Amazonia and the special people who live there, the more effective our struggle to save the planet will be.

e damos mirando, en ese entonces en la casi te
rente una señora estaba dando a luz, mientras
do jugaba al volley, aquí el tema de los hijos es muy
l tienen como 7 a 8 hijos incluso 12. y desde muy
tos, ayer mismo nos enteramos que una niña
ños está embarazada de 6 meses y por eso no ve
io. Hoy la tienda amaneció rodeada de termitas
ieron su camino atraves del techo, A veces
tienen muchos hijos se los regalan a otras familias
me contaba que tiene como 7 hijos, de los
2 hace como 2 años. o mas que no los ve, y
gual, También me pidió que le compre artesanias
ne haré y intentaré venderlas en ESPAÑA, y otras
balaré. Estos últimos días NO ESTOY COMIENDO MUCHO y
o UN PELIN DEBIL, LA COMIDA NO ES QUE SOBRE A us
LOS ALUMNOS LES TRAEN YUCA, PLATANO, ANANA,
VOSOTROS VAMOS UN POCO DE GORRONEO y a
GUSTA, TODAVÍA QUEDAN UNAS SOPAS ... ...
AZUCAR y ACEITE ... ...

(ESTE) KAI   MUNANGUICHU   RICUNATA ¿QUIERES MIRAR?
STOS: KAIGUNA   ARMANATA   BAÑAR
QUEL: PAI   PURINATA   CAMINAR
NUEVOS: PAIGUNA   NIKUNAK   comer
                                            PURIGUISHUN - PASEAR.
VA = IR
ngaremi = iré   ÁTUN = grande
cungacauni = miraré   RIMASHUN (HABLEMOS)

ui = chibi
ui = ceibi
Ri NAUDA chaina = de aquí a allí.
AMUI ¡VENGA!
amui vnikungawa
cu = vamos
vichi -

THANK YOU

To Ruth Muñiz for being who she is and for her inexhaustible struggle
to save the South American jungle and everything that lives in it.

To all the kids in the Sápara community of Conambo and to their
teachers Hernán and Vinicius.

To Michel, José Mari, Blanca, Anne, and Theo.

EPILOGUE

The Indigenous people say that in the jungle there are spirits amongst the trees and in the rivers, or that take the shapes of animals. Some tell that the harpy eagle, *chullwualy* in their language and the strongest eagle in the world, is a protector spirit. But all its strength is not enough if we can't find respect and admiration for all life within ourselves. We all have a little bit of the jungle inside us, whether we are in the city or in the jungle. Let us allow this most powerful spirit to grow and accompany us through our life and we will always have it with us.

Ruth Muñiz López
Chullwualy